In the fish bowl

written by Kim Faulkner

Illustrated by Corrina Rego

This book is dedicated to

Johnny, Adria, Sydney & Courtney

Maggie had a fish bowl with two pet gold fish.
Their names were Fred and Fran.

Fred and Fran would play in the bowl together all day long.
They were very happy, but one day something changed.

They saw Maggie come into the room with a clear plastic bag. She walked over to the bowl. She looked at her pet fish and said, "I have someone I want you to meet."

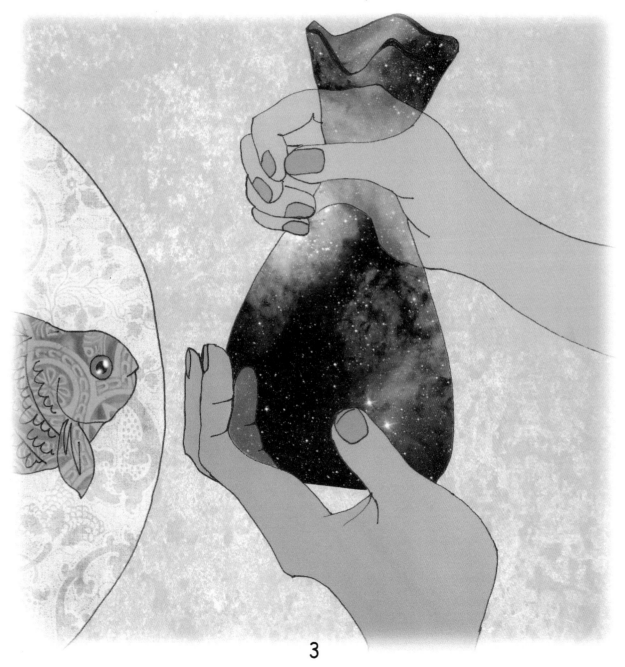

She poured the water from the bag into the bowl.
Out came a new kind of fish. "This is Mabel." said Maggie.
"My friend, Tim, is on vacation for a week and I told him
I would take care of Mabel. I hope you all will be friends."

Fred and Fran looked at Mabel. She did not look like them. Fred said,
"You should stay away from her. She's not like us, Fran."
So Fred and Fran continued to play together, without including Mabel.

Fred would say mean things about Mabel. He would say that she was ugly because she had whiskers and that her mouth was too big for a fish mouth. But, Fran thought to herself that Mabel didn't look that ugly. She was just different, bu Fred told Fran not to play with Mabel. Sometimes Mabel would hear things Fred would say and it made her sad.

One day, while Fred was sleeping, Fran swam over to Mabel. "Hi! I'm Fran. Welcome to our bowl. I'm a goldfish." "Hello," Mabel said with a smile "I'm a catfish." Mabel and Fran talked and played for a while. They became friends. Finally, Fran said "Fred will be awake from his nap soon. I should go back to the other side of the bowl now."

7

When Fred woke up Fran told him that she had been to meet Mabel. She explained to Fred that Mabel was a catfish and was very nice. Although she was different, Mabel and Fran had a whole lot of fun together. She told Fred he really should meet Mabel and get to know her.

8

Later that day, Fran told Fred that she was going over to play with Mabel some more. Fred was curious. Fred asked if he could go too.

Fran said, "Of course!" So Fred swam over with Fran.

He found out that Mabel was cool! She could use her big mouth to clean the bowl. Fred and Fran had to depend on Maggie to clean the bowl.

So every day the three fish would play together. Mabel showed that she coulc clean the bowl with her mouth. Fred and Fran totally forgot that Mabel was not like them. They were just three friends having fun.

Then one day Maggie came into the room with an empty plastic bag. "Say goodbye, Mabel. Tim is back from vacation and it is time to go home. Tim really missed you," said Maggie. Fred and Fran were sad that Maggie had to leave; they had become quite good friends. They told Mabel that she was welcome in their bowl anytime she wanted to visit. Mabel said the next time Tim went on vacation she would definitely come to see them.

11

Fred and Fran knew that the next time a new fish came to their bowl
they would try to be friends no matter what they looked like.

"This is My commandment,
that you love one another
as I have loved you."
John 15:12 (NKJV)

About the Author

Kim Faulkner is the author of *In the Fish Bowl*. She wrote this story when her son was in the 4th grade and she was inspired by her pet goldfish, Fred. She lives in Winston-Salem, NC with her wonderfully awesome family, her over active dog, two fish and a hamster. She is passionate about literacy and serves as a facilitator with the Next Chapter Book Club. Her dream is that one day no one will judge a book by its cover.

About the Illustrator

Corrina Rego, graphic designer and art teacher lives in sunny Bermuda with her happy little island family. Art is a language for her that she loves to share with everyone, be it in her class room or doing community projects. She believes we are all creative and loves to see that spark ignite in others!

55130389R00015

Made in the USA
Lexington, KY
16 September 2016